RANA

RANA RAIMAL, WHO RULED MEWAR IN THE EARLY HALF OF THE SIXTEENTH CENTURY, WAS A VALIANT KING WHO UPHELD THE GLORIOUS TRADITIONS OF HIS LAND. HIS THREE SONS, SANGA, PRITH-VIRAJ AND JAIMAL, HOWEVER, WERE FOR EVER INVOLVED IN PETTY QUARRELS WITH ONE ANOTHER.

THE DISUNITY OF OUR SONS WILL BE THE RUIN OF OUR KINGDOM.

BUT WHY DO THEY QUARREL SO?

1

EACH OF THEM WANTS TO BE MY SUCCESSOR.

BUT SANGA, THE ELDEST, HAS THE RIGHT TO THE THRONE.

THAT'S TRUE. THE PRINCES MIGHT HAVE ACCEPTED IT BUT FOR YOUR BROTHER, SURAJMAL. HE SETS THEM AGAINST ONE ANOTHER.

I CAN'T UNDERSTAND WHY HE DOES IT.

WHILE RAIMAL WORRIED, THE PRINCES CONTINUED TO QUARREL AND DRAW THEIR SWORDS AT THE SLIGHTEST PRETEXT.

I AM A BORN LEADER— BORN TO BE THE RULER OF MEWAR.

UNFORTUNATELY I AM THE RIGHTFUL HEIR, PRITHVIRAJ.

RIGHTFUL PERHAPS—BUT YOU ARE NOT FIT TO RULE, SANGA.

WHO SAYS SO?

I DO!

BEFORE SANGA COULD SAY ANYTHING, SURAJMAL CUT IN—

YOU FORGET ONE THING, PRITHVIRAJ— YOU HAVE NOT TAKEN INTO ACCOUNT THE WISHES OF THE PEOPLE.

WHAT CHANCE DO THE WISHES OF THE PEOPLE HAVE AGAINST MY MIGHT?

AS SANGA WAS ABOUT TO REPLY—

LET THE ORACLE, CHARANI DEVI, GUIDE US. HER PREDICTIONS NEVER GO WRONG.

THEY MOUNTED THEIR HORSES...

...AND SOON ARRIVED AT THE TEMPLE OF CHARANI DEVI.

WE HAVE COME TO CONSULT CHARANI DEVI.

WHAT DO YOU WANT TO KNOW?

WE'D LIKE TO KNOW WHICH OF US IS DESTINED TO RULE MEWAR.

PLEASE SIT DOWN. I WILL PUT THE QUESTION TO THE DEVI. SHE WILL GIVE YOU THE ANSWER THROUGH HER ATTENDANT.

SANGA, IF THE PREDICTION IS NOT IN YOUR FAVOUR, WHAT WILL YOU DO?

THE CALM AND PEACE OF THE TEMPLE HAD A STRANGE EFFECT ON SANGA. HE NO LONGER WANTED TO FIGHT WITH HIS BROTHERS.

I WILL GO AWAY AND ESTABLISH A NEW KINGDOM ELSEWHERE, IF MEWAR IS NOT DESTINED TO BE MINE.

AND IF IT IS, YOU WILL HAVE TO KILL ME FIRST.

5

MEANWHILE, THE PRIEST RETURNED WITH THE ATTENDANT WHO WAS THE MOUTHPIECE OF THE DEVI.

HERE THEY COME— WITH THE PREDICTION!

THE ATTENDANT POINTED TO THE TIGER SKIN ON WHICH SANGA WAS SITTING AND SURAJMAL WAS RESTING A KNEE.

THAT MEANS I AM TO RULE THE KINGDOM...

...OF WHICH I WILL ENJOY A SHARE.

SO THAT WAS THE JACKAL'S GAME!

6

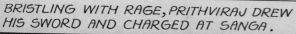

BRISTLING WITH RAGE, PRITHVIRAJ DREW HIS SWORD AND CHARGED AT SANGA.

I WILL KILL THE LION FIRST AND THEN TACKLE THE JACKAL.

BUT SURAJMAL WHO LEAPT FORWARD TO PARRY THE THRUST...

...RECEIVED THE BLOW.

WHEN SANGA SAW THIS—

I WILL NOT INVOLVE MYSELF IN A FIGHT WITH MY BROTHER— AND CERTAINLY NOT IN THIS TEMPLE.

HE RAN OUT...

...AND MOUNTED HIS HORSE.

STOP SANGA! OR I'LL SHOOT YOU DOWN.

PRITHVIRAJ PULLED OUT AN ARROW AND TOOK AIM.

THE ARROW HIT SANGA IN ONE EYE, BLINDING IT FOR LIFE.

AH!

AS PRITHVIRAJ WAS ABOUT TO RUN UP TO SANGA AND FINISH HIM —

PRITHVIRAJ! STOP IT! FOR GOD'S SAKE!

THEN I WILL TAKE CARE OF YOU FIRST, UNCLE!

MEANWHILE —

PRITHVIRAJ'S ATTENTION IS DIVERTED. I'D BETTER ESCAPE.

WITH GREAT DIFFICULTY SANGA MANAGED TO REMOUNT HIS HORSE. AS HE WAS ABOUT TO RIDE AWAY —

JAIMAL! GO AFTER SANGA! DON'T LET HIM GET AWAY ALIVE!

DON'T WORRY, PRITHVIRAJ. I'LL FINISH HIM.

SANGA, STOP! I SAY STOP.

AT THAT MOMENT, VEEDA, A TRADESMAN WHO WAS PREPARING TO GO OUT OF MEWAR, WAS TAKING LEAVE OF HIS FAMILY. SUDDENLY—

THE PRINCES! THEY ARE COMING THIS WAY.

A FEW SECONDS LATER, UNABLE TO RIDE FURTHER, SANGA CAME TO A HALT IN FRONT OF VEEDA.

PRINCE SANGA! YOU ARE BADLY WOUNDED!

VEEDA HELPED SANGA DISMOUNT AND TURNED TO HIS WIFE—

QUICK! LEAD HIM TO MY HORSE, WHICH IS TIED BEHIND THE HOUSE. I'LL HANDLE JAIMAL.

A FEW SECONDS AFTER VEEDA'S WIFE LED SANGA AWAY, JAIMAL RODE UP.

WHERE IS SANGA?

I'LL GIVE UP MY LIFE BUT I'LL NEVER TELL YOU.

ENRAGED, JAIMAL DREW HIS SWORD AND ATTACKED VEEDA.

THIS SHOULD GIVE PRINCE SANGA ENOUGH TIME TO GET AWAY.

VEEDA STOPPED JAIMAL BUT AT THE COST OF HIS LIFE.

-11-

SANGA, MEANWHILE, ESCAPED ON VEEDA'S HORSE.

I WILL NOT GO BACK. PRITHVIRAJ IS DETERMINED TO TAKE THE THRONE. OUR WAR OVER THE SUCCESSION WILL BENEFIT NONE BUT THE ENEMIES OF MEWAR.

SO SANGA RODE AWAY FROM CHITTOR TOWARDS THE JUNGLES.

A FEW HOURS LATER, SANGA SAW SOME SHEPHERDS. HE APPROACHED THEM FOR WORK.

CAN YOU GRAZE OUR GOATS AND SHEEP AND COOK FOR US?

I WILL TRY.

AS A MENIAL, SANGA, THE PRINCE, WAS A FAILURE.

HE IS A GOOD-FOR-NOTHING!

IT'S NO USE KEEPING HIM.

FROM HIS WOUNDS I WOULD SAY HE IS A RUN-AWAY BANDIT.

SANGA SOON BECAME SICK AND TIRED OF THEIR STEADY ABUSE.

I MUST FIND SOME OTHER EMPLOYMENT.

BUT NOTHING CAME HIS WAY.

A FEW DAYS LATER—

ARMED HORSEMEN! THEY SEEM TO BE REBEL RAJPUTS.

WHO ARE YOU?

THEY HAVEN'T RECOGNISED ME. SHALL I ASK THEM TO GIVE ME SOME ARMS?

MY NAME IS SANGRAM SINGH. I TOO AM A RAJPUT. BUT I HAVE NO ARMS EVEN FOR MY OWN PROTECTION.

WE'LL GIVE YOU ARMS. WHY DON'T YOU JOIN US?

WITH PLEASURE!

MY LUCK SEEMS TO HAVE TURNED.

COME, THEN. WE'LL TAKE YOU TO OUR CHIEF.

SANGA WAS INTRODUCED TO THEIR CHIEF, KARAM CHAND.

THIS BRAVE RAJPUT, SANGRAM SINGH, WISHES TO WORK WITH US.

LET'S HOPE YOU MAKE A GOOD DACOIT.

OH! SO THEY'RE REBELS WHO HAVE TURNED DACOITS.

AS SANGA HESITATED, KARAM CHAND'S DAUGHTER CAME OUT—

TAKE SANGRAM IN AND ATTEND TO HIS NEEDS.

YES, FATHER.

SANGA AND KARAM CHAND'S DAUGHTER SOON FELL IN LOVE WITH EACH OTHER. ONE DAY—

WHAT ARE YOU DOING HERE ALONE?

THINKING!

WHAT ARE YOU THINKING ABOUT?

I DO NOT LIKE THE LIFE I'M LEADING.

NEITHER DO I.

THEN WHY DON'T YOU MARRY ME AND COME AWAY WITH ME?

MARU, ONE OF THE REBELS, OVERHEARD THEIR CONVERSATION AND TOLD KARAM CHAND ABOUT IT.

SO SANGRAM HAS NO TASTE FOR OUR WAY OF LIFE. HM.M..!

KARAM CHAND ASKED MARU TO KEEP A CLOSE WATCH ON SANGA. A FEW DAYS LATER—

WHAT IS IT, MARU?

COME OUT AND SEE FOR YOURSELF, SIR. IT'S UNBELIEVABLE!

SO YOU HAVE BEEN MEETING EACH OTHER!

YES. WE HAVE. I WANT TO MARRY HER.

YOU HAVE MY CONSENT BUT PROMISE ME YOU WILL NOT MAKE HER UNHAPPY.

YOU CAN TRUST ME.

AFTER THE WEDDING, SANGA AND HIS BRIDE APPROACHED KARAM CHAND FOR HIS BLESSINGS.

SANGRAM, I APPOINT YOU NAIK OF MY BAND.

I CANNOT ACCEPT. I AM DESTINED TO RULE OVER MEWAR.

RULE OVER MEWAR! ISN'T THAT A VAIN HOPE?

NOT FOR RANA SANGA, THE ELDEST SON OF RANA RAIMAL!

RANA SANGA?

YES. I AM RANA SANGA. BUT I WANT YOU TO KEEP MY SECRET AND GIVE ME PROTECTION TILL I KNOW WHAT THE SITUATION IS LIKE IN CHITTOR.

WE WILL SEND SOMEONE TO FIND OUT.

THE MESSENGER RETURNED WITH INTERESTING NEWS. SANGA'S BAD DAYS WERE OVER. PRITHVIRAJ AND JAIMAL WERE NO MORE.

THE KING'S MEN ARE LOOKING FOR YOU EVERYWHERE.

GO TO CHITTOR. DON'T WASTE ANOTHER MOMENT.

MEANWHILE, AT CHITTOR—

TWO SONS KILLED, AND SANGA NOT YET TRACED.

WHO WILL SUCCEED ME? WHAT WILL BECOME OF MY KINGDOM.

HAVE PATIENCE, SIR. OUR MEN ARE LOOKING EVERYWHERE FOR...

AT THAT MOMENT—

MAHARAJ KI JAI! PRINCE SANGA IS HERE!

MY SON! WHERE IS MY SON?

WHERE IS HE?

GOD HAS GRANTED OUR PRAYERS!

SON, WHERE WERE YOU ALL THIS TIME?

WHAT DOES IT MATTER? HE IS HERE NOW.

YES. I AM HERE, ALIVE AND WELL!

SOON AFTERWARDS, RAIMAL DIED AND SANGA BECAME KING. WITHIN A FEW YEARS, MEWAR REACHED THE SUMMIT OF PROSPERITY. ONE DAY AT COURT—

IBRAHIM LODI'S POWER IS ALREADY ON THE DECLINE.

WE CAN VANQUISH THE SULTAN WITHOUT MUCH DIFFICULTY!

TO WIN DELHI IS TO RULE THE WHOLE COUNTRY!

SULTAN, I WILL NOT LET YOU ESCAPE!

THE SULTAN WAS SOON CAPTURED.

HIS ARMY HAD FLED.

THOUGH A PRISONER, MAHMOOD KHILJI WAS TREATED LIKE AN HONOURED GUEST.

WHY DO YOU TREAT ME, A PRISONER, SO ROYALLY?

BECAUSE YOU ARE A KING AND A GUEST IN MY PALACE.

I COULD EASILY ESCAPE.

THAT WOULD BE COWARDLY.

KHILJI HAD TO CEDE FOUR PROVINCES — BHILSA, SARANGPUR, CHANDERI AND RANTHAMBOR — BEFORE SANGA RELEASED HIM. MEANWHILE, BABAR HAD INVADED DELHI.

BABAR IS JUST ANOTHER PLUNDERER!

IF HE DEFEATS LODI, HE WILL COLLECT ALL THE WEALTH HE CAN AND GO BACK!

AND IF HE STAYS ON, IT WON'T MAKE ANY DIFFERENCE TO US.

HIS NEW REGIME WILL NOT BE STRONG ENOUGH TO RESIST US.

WHETHER WE FIGHT LODI OR BABAR — IT IS ALL THE SAME TO US.

WE MUST TAKE OVER DELHI AT ALL COSTS.

IN APRIL 1526, BABAR DEFEATED IBRAHIM LODI, BECAME THE NEW RULER OF DELHI AND IMMEDIATELY MADE PREPARATIONS FOR A WAR ON CHITTOR. SANGA HELD COUNCIL WITH HIS MINISTERS.

AMAZING! BABAR HAS COMPLETED HIS PREPARATIONS!

HE SEEMS TO BE AMBITIOUS.

ALL BRAVE MEN ARE AMBITIOUS. SHILADITYA, OUR FORCES HAVE TO BE FURTHER STRENGTHENED.

HE SHOULD BE DRIVEN OUT OF OUR MOTHERLAND.

I LIKE YOUR SPIRIT, SHILADITYA. I PUT YOU IN CHARGE OF THE DEFENCE UNITS.

WE TRUST YOU TO PERFORM YOUR TASK WITH HONOUR AND SINCERITY.

I WILL NOT HESITATE TO LAY DOWN MY LIFE IN DOING MY DUTY.

MEANWHILE, AT BABAR'S COURT IN DELHI—

JAHANPANAH, WE WILL RUN A GREAT RISK IN FIGHTING RANA SANGA.

OUR SOLDIERS ARE OVERAWED BY THE VALOUR OF THE RAJPUTS.

LET US TEST THE METTLE OF THIS MAN WHO HAS ONLY ONE EYE AND ONE ARM.

IN MARCH 1527, BABAR ATTACKED. THE FORCES OF RANA SANGA AND BABAR MET IN THE BATTLEFIELD OF KHANWA.

BABAR'S ADVANCE OF ABOUT 1500 MEN WAS CUT TO PIECES.

REINFORCEMENTS WERE SENT BUT THEY TOO MADE A HURRIED RETREAT.

JAHANPANAH, OUR SOLDIERS HAVE ALREADY LOST HEART.

I WILL SPEAK TO THEM.

BABAR ORDERED THE DESTRUCTION OF ALL WINE FLASKS.

I VOW NEVER TO DRINK WINE AGAIN.

THEN HE MADE A STIRRING SPEECH BEFORE HIS SOLDIERS.

...BY THE HOLY KORAN, VICTORY WILL BE OURS.

I HOPE I DO NOT HAVE TO SUE FOR PEACE.

ON THE SECOND DAY OF THE BATTLE, HOWEVER, BABAR SENT HIS EMISSARY TO RANA SANGA.

WE WILL ACCEPT BABAR'S PEACE PROPOSAL— ON OUR TERMS.

BUT BABAR REJECTED THE TERMS. A LITTLE LATER—

JEHANPANAH, RANA SANGA'S EMISSARY IS HERE.

BRING HIM IN WITH DUE HONOUR.

ACCEPT OUR TERMS. IT IS NOT POSSIBLE TO DEFEAT SANGA'S ARMY.

YOU CAN MAKE IT POSSIBLE.

WHAT DO YOU MEAN?

IF WE JOIN HANDS, WE CAN BOTH GET WHAT WE WANT!

YOU MEAN YOU WIN THE WAR.

AND YOU GET CHITTOR!

GREED GOT THE BETTER OF SHILADITYA.

YOU WON'T GO BACK ON YOUR WORD, WILL YOU?

ON THE HOLY KORAN — I WILL NOT.

AS SOON AS SHILADITYA RETURNED TO HIS CAMP—

THE RANA HAS BEEN ASKING FOR YOU.

I'LL GO TO HIM.

IS MY SECRET ALREADY KNOWN?

PARDON ME, MAHARAJ — I WAS DELAYED.

EVERY PASSING MOMENT IS PRECIOUS!

BABAR HAS REJECTED OUR TERMS.

TOMORROW WE ATTACK. THE BATTLE WILL BE FOUGHT IN THAT VALLEY. WE WILL MOUNT A TWO-PRONGED ATTACK.

THERE OUR ARMY WILL FIGHT THE ENEMY FACE TO FACE; AND WE WILL ATTACK THE REAR-GUARD FROM THAT HILL.

OUR FRONTAL ATTACK MUST BE STRONG OTHERWISE THE ENEMY WILL MARCH STRAIGHT TO CHITTOR.

BOTH ARMIES ARE GETTING READY.

MOTHER CHANDI IS MY WITNESS — WE WILL WIN.

THIS WILL BE THE DECISIVE DAY.

THE TWO ARMIES SOON FACED EACH OTHER.

SUDDENLY—

LOOK! LOOK! INSTEAD OF FIGHTING, THE TWO ARMIES ARE MARCHING TOWARDS CHITTOR TOGETHER.

WE HAVE BEEN BETRAYED. SHILADITYA, I TRUSTED YOU...

SINCE THE MAJOR PART OF HIS ARMY HAD BEEN GIVEN TO SHILADITYA, RANA SANGA HAD TO ABANDON HIS PLANS.

A REAR ATTACK WOULD NOW BE IN VAIN.

RANA SANGA AND HIS MEN WANDERED INTO THE HILLS, AWAITING AN OPPORTUNITY TO ATTACK THE MUGHALS.

I VOW NOT TO RETURN TO MEWAR UNTIL I'VE VANQUISHED THE MUGHALS.

WE ARE WITH YOU.

BUT THE UNCERTAINTY AND INSECURITY OF LIFE IN EXILE AFFECTED THE RANA'S HEALTH.

HE WAS CONFINED TO BED AND WAS UNABLE TO FULFIL HIS VOW.

WILL YOU FORGIVE YOUR DEFAULTING SON, O MOTHER-LAND?

A FEW MONTHS LATER, HE DIED AT VASVA, A VILLAGE IN THE HILLS.

IF SHILADITYA HAD NOT BETRAYED RANA SANGA, INDIA PERHAPS WOULD HAVE BEEN SAVED THE HUMILIATION OF FOREIGN DOMINATION.